HANDS-ON HISTORY

PROJECTS ABOUT

The Spanish West

David C. King

Marshall Cavendish
Benchmark
New York

Marshall Cavendish Benchmark
99 White Plains Road
Tarrytown, NY 10591-9001
www.marshallcavendish.us

Library of Congress Cataloging-in-Publication Data

King, David C.
 Projects about the Spanish West / by David C. King.
    p. cm.— (Hands-on history)
 Summary: "Social studies projects reflecting Spanish culture on the American West"—Provided by publisher.
 Includes bibliographical references and index.
 ISBN 0-7614-1982-9 (alk. paper)
 1. Spanish Americans—Southwest, New—Social life and customs—Study and teaching—Activity programs—Juvenile literature. 2. Spaniards South-
west, New—Social life and customs—Study and teaching—Activity programs—Juvenile literature. 3. Hispanic Americans—Southwest, New—Social
life and customs—Study and teaching—Activity programs—Juvenile literature. 4. Southwest, New—Social life and customs—Study and teaching—
Activity programs—Juvenile literature.

I. Title. II. Series.

F790.S75K56 2005979'00468073--dc22
2005004770

Maps and illustrations by Rodica Prato

Title Page: The Mission San Diego de Alcala was founded on July 16, 1769.
Photo research by Joan Meisel
Photo credits: *Alamy*:Blake Shaw, 16. *Art Resource, NY*: Manu Sassooncan, 10. *Corbis*: Reinhard Eisele, 1; Buddy Mays, 13; Jan Butchofsky-Houser, 20;
Dave G. Houser, 24; Danny Lehman, 34; David Seawell, 38. *Getty Images*: Hulton Archive, 4; Photodisc Blue, 6; Photodisc Green, 23; Mary Ellen Bart-
ley/FoodPix, 7. *North Wind Picture Archive*: 8. *Photo Researchers, Inc.*:Lawrence Migdale, 28, 39.

Printed in China

1 3 5 6 4 2

Contents

In 1541, Spanish explorer Francisco Vasquez de Coronado's expedition crossed the American Southwest.

1

Introduction

❧

The American Southwest is a beautiful region of deserts and mountains that covers all of Arizona and New Mexico, plus parts of California, Utah, Nevada, Colorado, and Texas. This sun-filled land has been home to American Indian tribes for thousands of years. The Navajo, Hopi, and Zuni tribes lived by farming. They grew crops of corn, beans, squash, and sunflowers. Hunting, fishing, and gathering wild foods added to their diet.

About five hundred years ago, newcomers arrived. They were from the European nation of Spain. In the century following the voyages of Christopher Columbus, the Spanish built a mighty empire that stretched from Mexico to the tip of South America.

Spanish explorers named the Rio Grande, which means "Great River."

Mixing Languages

When the Spanish arrived in the Southwest, they used their own language to describe the majestic snow-capped mountains and the surprisingly colorful deserts. The river they crossed to reach the Southwest they named the Rio Grande (Spanish for "Great River"). They called one desert region Arizona, meaning "dry or arid zone." And for the more colorful landscape of Colorado, they used a name that means "a state of color." They also used Spanish names for towns like Santa Fe, which means "Holy Faith."

In the mid-1500s, the Spanish moved north from Mexico into what is now the American Southwest. They brought a very different culture, or way of life, as well as animals that the Indians had never seen before. The Indians also learned about new foods including oranges, lemons, apples, wheat, and oats.

The coming together of the Spanish and Native Americans created a remarkable mixing of cultures. In this book, you'll discover some of the ways the Spanish shaped life in the Southwest. You'll learn to use wool yarn to make a picture and to create a punched-tin lantern to light a path during a celebration. You can also try making a delicious Spanish dessert or playing a homemade banjo.

This illustration of a mission in California shows some of the people that could be found in and around such settlements—missionaries, Spanish soldiers, and Native Americans.

2

Spanish Craftspeople

The Spanish were sure that they were meant to rule the lands and people of the Southwest. They wanted to make the Native Americans give up their beliefs and become Christians, and to teach them the European way of life. But the Native Americans were fiercely independent and proud of their traditional ways. Villages or tribes sometimes joined together to fight for independence from Spanish rule.

In the 1600s, a revolt by the Pueblo Indians drove the Spanish out of Santa Fe and back to Mexico. The Pueblos' independence did not last. Cooperation among the Pueblos weakened, and the Spanish gradually got control again.

Some Spanish immigrants moved into the mountains, partly to avoid conflict with the Indians and partly for the mountains' great beauty and privacy. Thousands of their descendants continue to live in those rugged hills today. They grow some crops and raise a few sheep and goats. They also earn money from their crafts—painting on wood or tin, carving wood, and making things out of wool, cotton, or leather. The products of the Spanish craftspeople are popular with tourists, and their work is sold throughout the Southwest.

This yarn painting was created by a Huichol Indian artist. The Huichol live in the Sierra Madre Mountains of Mexico.

Yarn Picture

You are traveling through New Mexico with your family during summer vacation. At the public square in Santa Fe, you meet two twelve-year-old girls who are working together to make a large picture of a cat out of colorful strands of yarn. They explain that early Spanish craftspeople used wool in many ways. Southwestern Indians learned these techniques from the Spanish. The girls invite you to make one of the pictures. One girl explains that the pictures are called **ofrendas,** a word that means "offerings" or "gifts." Years ago, artists pressed the yarn into soft wax spread over a thin board. For your *ofrenda,* you'll push the yarn into a thin coat of white glue. Yarn paintings usually show a bird or animal, but they sometimes are of plants and abstract designs.

You will need:

- 2 or 3 sheets of newspaper
- ruler
- pencil

- stiff cardboard, about 8 1/2 by 11 inches
- scissors
- white glue or craft glue
- yarn, in several bright colors

Tip: Use dark colors to outline the cat and for important parts like the face.

---

1. Spread the newspapers over your work surface and arrange the materials on top.

2. With the ruler and pencil, make a 6 by 8 inch rectangle on the cardboard. Use the scissors to cut it out.

3. Draw an outline of your picture on the rectangle. Use the cat shown here or choose another idea—an animal, a plant, or your own design.

4. Spread glue in a thin line along the outline of your picture. Place a piece of yarn along the glue, and press gently. To keep the yarn fluffy, handle it as little as possible.

5. Continue putting down glue and then yarn. Start a new piece where the last one ended.

6. Using different colors, however you like, fill the entire picture in the same way. Make the colors as bright as possible. Use small pieces to fill in any spaces.

7. Fill in the background. First, add one or two single pieces all the way around the edge of the cardboard. Then work your way toward the picture with one solid color, as shown in blue.

Carving

An elderly Spaniard is sitting on the steps of his cabin, which is located high in the mountains above Taos, New Mexico. He is a wood carver. This craft is something his family has done for hundreds of years.

"In the early years here," he says, "Spanish artists painted pictures on pieces of tin or copper. We are very religious people, so nearly all our paintings were of holy subjects, like Jesus or the Virgin Mary. These paintings were called *retablos.*

"Then, my great-grandfather and other artists changed from painting to wood carving. They thought that the carvings would be a better way for people to understand what a holy person looks like."

The carvings are called *santos* because most are wood sculptures of saints. Because they are three-dimensional, people can turn them around and see them from different sides. The figures vary from a few inches to 4 or 5 feet long. They are painted in bright colors with details in black.

Wood carvers make their *santos* from pine. You can use Sculpey, which is soft and easy to carve. If you prefer, you can make your carving out of a bar of soap.

Two examples of wooden santos.

13

1. Choose a subject for your carving—a person, a comic-book character, or copy the drawing of a *santos*. Or you could carve a favorite animal; a piece of fruit, like a pear or an apple; or a tree or plant. With the pencil, sketch a rough outline of your subject on each side of the block of Sculpey or soap. Cut away the excess.

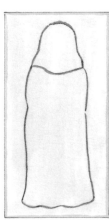

2. Place the block of Sculpey or soap on a cutting board or magazine.

3. Using the knife or tool, work slowly and carefully to cut away the extra Sculpey or soap. Cut off small amounts. Turn the carving often to make your figure as round as possible. Ask an adult to help you if you have trouble.

4. If you've carved your figure in Sculpey, follow the manufacturer's directions for baking it in the oven.

5. When it's done, take it out of the oven with pot holders and let it cool.

6. When it's completely dry and cool, paint your *santo,* or other object, in bright colors. Use the marker to add details, like the face.

Ojos de dios souvenirs on display.

Ojo de Dios

A brother and sister in a small Arizona town are making decorations out of wood and yarn. The decorations are called **ojo de Dios** (pronounced o-ho day DEE-ohs), a Spanish term that means eye of God. "The decorations are for good luck," the girl explains, "and they look neat on the wall."

Her brother continues: "A Spanish wood carver from the mountains came to our school and showed us how to make the *ojo de Dios.* He said that a long time ago these were made for a Spanish festival in October, but now people use them for Christmas, New Year's, and other holidays."

You can use your *ojo de Dios* as a wall hanging, a holiday decoration, or a gift.

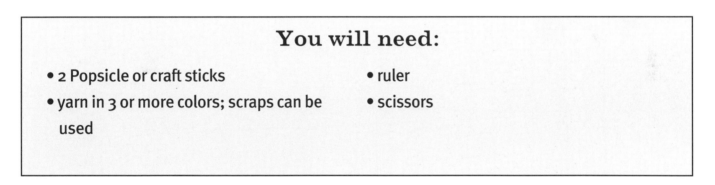

You will need:

- 2 Popsicle or craft sticks
- yarn in 3 or more colors; scraps can be used
- ruler
- scissors

1. Make the sticks into a cross. Tie one end of a piece of yarn (about 12 inches long) to one of the dowels close to where it meets the other dowels, then wind it around the center as shown. Wind the yarn tightly so it will bind the crosspieces together. The winding forms a small bump, two or three strands thick. Wood carvers call this bump the *ojo,* or "eye."

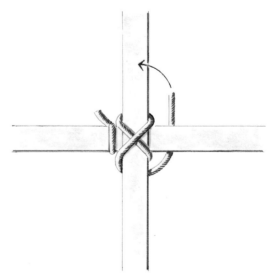

2. Choose a different color for the second strand and tie it to the first strand. If possible, tie the knot close to the crosspiece, so you can tuck it behind.

3. Wind the second strand once around the crosspiece, then take it to the next crosspiece, wind it once, and continue all the way around.

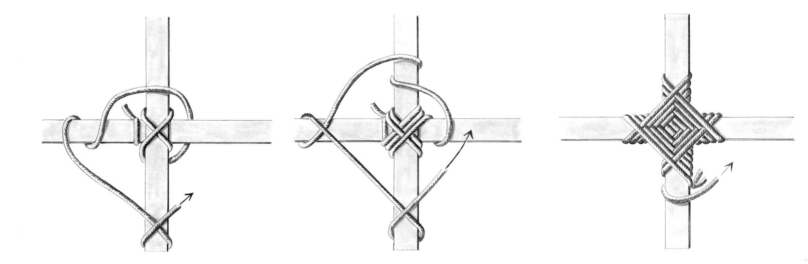

4. Go around two or three more times. Cut the second strand, tie on a new strand of a different color.

5. Continue winding strands and changing colors every time you've gone around once or twice. When you tie on a new strand, try to hide the knot behind a crosspiece or tuck it into another strand. When only 1½ to 2 inches of the sticks remain uncovered, stop winding and tie the last piece of yarn to a crosspiece.

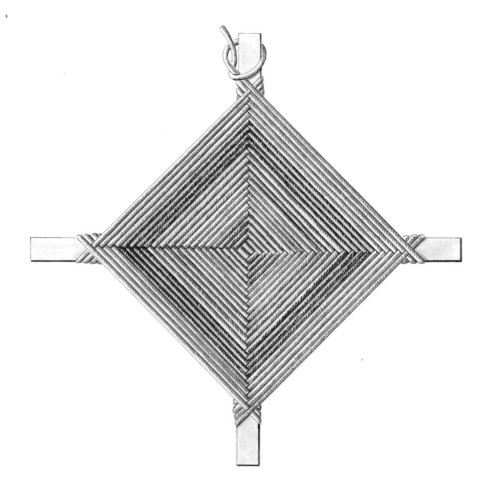

A woman strings chilies at a living history museum in Santa Fe, New Mexico.

3

Foods: Old World and New

❧

One of the most remarkable results of the meeting of Spanish and Indian cultures was the blending of foods from the **Old World** of Europe, Asia, and Africa, and the **New World** of North and South America. The Native Americans, like all New World peoples, knew nothing about the foods brought by the Spanish. The Europeans were just as surprised to learn about foods like corn, tomatoes, and chocolate. The recipes in this chapter use foods from both worlds.

The Origins of Foods

Roughly half the foods we eat today came from the Old World and half from the New. Below is a brief list of foods from both worlds. Make a list of all the foods you eat in one day. Try to figure out if they are old or new world foods by looking them up in an encyclopedia.

Old World Foods

Grains	Fruits and Vegetables	Animal Products	Other
oats	apples	beef	coffee
rice	apricots	chickens	milk
rye	grapes	goats	sugar
wheat	lemons		tea
	oranges		
	peas		

New World Foods

Fruits and Vegetables		Animal Products	Other
avocados	pineapples	turkey	chocolate
beans	potatoes		maple syrup
corn	pumpkins		
grapefruits	squash		
limes	tomatoes		

Huevos Rancheros (Tortillas and Eggs)

The year is 1891. On a cattle ranch in southern Colorado, a woman and her daughter are preparing breakfast for four hungry ranch workers. "My great-grandparents used this recipe when they first started the ranch," the woman says. "That was just after all this land became part of the United States. The recipe is quick, tasty, and filling—perfect for hungry young men."

1. Make the tortillas. Mix the flour, baking powder, and salt in the large mixing bowl with the large spoon.

2. Add the butter or shortening and the water.

3. Mix the dough with your hands until it forms a ball. Cover the bowl with the dish towel and leave for ten to fifteen minutes.

4. Break off a piece of dough. On a lightly floured countertop or pastry board, roll out the piece of dough into a small thin circle, about 6 inches across. Do the same with the rest of the dough, making four or five circles in all.

5. Heat the ungreased frying pan over medium heat. Cook one tortilla at a time, turning once or twice with the pancake turner until the dough is lightly browned on both sides.

6. Place the cooked tortillas on the plate or serving platter and cover with the dish towel. Set the tortillas aside.

7. Warm the corn oil in the frying pan.

8. Break the eggs into the small bowl and stir with the fork. Pour the eggs into the frying pan and stir as they cook. Use the pancake turner to keep them from sticking.

9. When the eggs are done, put a tortilla on the platter, place some of the eggs on the tortilla, cover the egg with some salsa, then roll up the tortilla. Continue with the rest of the tortillas.

10. Serve warm, with extra salsa on the side.

Capirotada (Mexican Bread Pudding)

This recipe was brought to the Southwest by early Spanish settlers. All the ingredients came from Europe, Asia, and the Pacific Islands.

Capirotada makes a great dessert. The Spanish called it spotted dog—you will be able to figure out why.

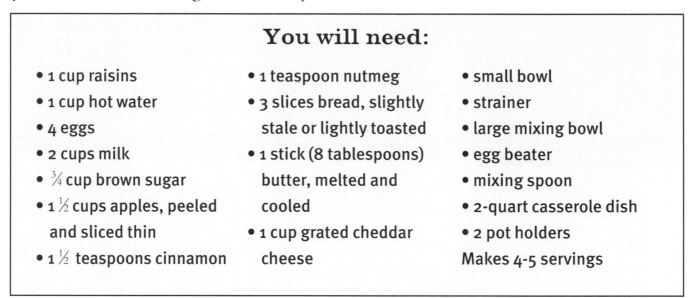

You will need:

- 1 cup raisins
- 1 cup hot water
- 4 eggs
- 2 cups milk
- ¾ cup brown sugar
- 1 ½ cups apples, peeled and sliced thin
- 1 ½ teaspoons cinnamon
- 1 teaspoon nutmeg
- 3 slices bread, slightly stale or lightly toasted
- 1 stick (8 tablespoons) butter, melted and cooled
- 1 cup grated cheddar cheese
- small bowl
- strainer
- large mixing bowl
- egg beater
- mixing spoon
- 2-quart casserole dish
- 2 pot holders

Makes 4-5 servings

1. Ask an adult for help. Preheat the oven to 350 degrees.

2. Put the raisins into a small bowl and pour the hot water over them. Let the raisins soak about three minutes. Over the sink, pour the raisins into the strainer. Rest the strainer full of raisins in the small bowl so it doesn't leak. Set aside.

3. Break the eggs into a large bowl and beat them well with the egg beater. Add the milk and stir well. Add the brown sugar next and stir. Make sure the sugar doesn't form clumps. Then mix in the apples, cinnamon, and nutmeg.

4. Break the bread into small pieces, and add it to the egg-and-milk mixture. Stir in the melted butter, add the raisins, and mix thoroughly with the spoon.

5. Pour half the mixture into a 2-quart casserole dish. Sprinkle half the cheese over the top. Pour the rest of the egg-and-milk mixture into the casserole then cover that with the rest of the cheese.

6. Bake for forty-five minutes. Remove the casserole from the oven with pot holders, and let it cool on top of the stove for a few minutes. Serve warm.

Children in traditional costumes perform at a Cinco de Mayo festival in San Jose, California.

4
Festivals

Some of the earliest Spaniards to reach the Southwest were **missionaries.** The missionaries were Catholic priests who came to the New World to bring Christianity to all Native American peoples. The Spanish built beautiful churches and cathedrals throughout South America and Mexico. When they moved into the American Southwest, they built missions—places where they could teach Indians about Christianity and also show them new ways of farming and making things.

Over the next four hundred years, many of the people of the Southwest became Catholics. Others kept their traditional Indian religions. Many combined the two in their celebrations and festivals.

Party Piñata

Making piñatas began in Italy in the fifteenth century. The Spanish then started to make them and brought them to the New World. In the American Southwest, the piñatas were made with three cones on top. Piñatas were made for the **Feast of the Three Kings**—a Church celebration held in early January. The cones represented the Three Kings (or Wise Men) who brought gifts to the infant Jesus. Indian children believed that the Three Kings filled the cones with presents that spilled out when the piñata was broken open.

Piñatas were originally made of thin clay, but you'll be following the modern technique of working with papier-mâché. This project is a lot of fun but, because of the drying time, it takes four or five days to complete. You should also know that working with papier-mâché can be pretty messy, so you'll want to wear an apron or a smock.

You will need:

- several sheets of newspaper
- large bowl
- ¼–½ cup flour
- 4 cups of water
- 2 tablespoons salt
- round balloon
- scissors
- about 3 feet of string
- ruler
- pencil
- 1 sheet construction paper, any color
- craft knife
- 20-30 small prizes (small toys or wrapped candy)
- colored tissue paper
- white glue or craft glue
- tempera or acrylic paint,
- paintbrush, and jar of water, optional
- mixing spoon
- Scotch tape

1. Spread several sheets of newspaper over your work surface. In the large bowl, make paste by mixing the flour and the water with the spoon until the liquid looks like thick glue. Add more water or flour as necessary. Mix well to get out all the lumps. Add the salt to help prevent mold.

2. Blow up the balloon until it is 8 to10 inches from top to bottom, then tie it.

3. Tear two or three other sheets of newspaper into small strips—each about 1 by 4 inches. Dip the strips of newspaper, one by one, into the paste. Remove extra paste by running each strip between your first and middle fingers. Place each strip on the balloon, overlapping the strips. When the balloon is covered, add a second layer of pasted strips, placing them in a different direction.

4. Make a harness for the piñata. Cut two 12-inch pieces of string. Tie one over the middle of the other so they form a cross. Place the balloon on top of where the two strings meet. Bring the four ends of string up and tie them together. Tape the strings to the sides of the balloon to hold them in place. Attach a long piece of string at the top for hanging the piñata.

5. Paste on two more layers of newspaper strips, covering the taped strings. Hang the piñata to dry. The drying time will be three or four days.

6. Make the three cones. With the ruler and pencil, measure a circle that is eight inches across on the construction paper. Cut it out. Divide the circle into four pie-shaped quarters. Form three of these pie-shaped pieces into cones, as in the drawing. Hold the seams closed with Scotch tape. Tape the cones to the sides of the balloon, about a third of the way from the top of the balloon.

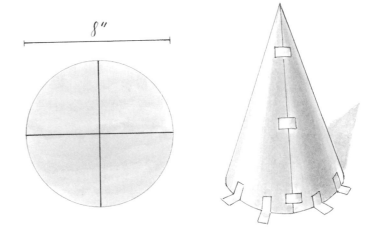

7. With an adult's help, use a craft knife or a point of the scissors to cut three sides of a small trapdoor, about 3 by 3 inches, near the top of the balloon. This will pop the balloon. If you can, pull out the balloon—or you can let it fall to the bottom.

8. Cut the tissue paper into strips, about 3 inches wide and 7 or 8 inches long. Place several strips on top of each other and cut fringes in them, as shown.

9. Add single layers of fringe to the piñata. Squeeze a little white glue or craft glue onto the solid part of each fringe. Begin at the bottom of the piñata, with the cut edges facing down. Overlap the pieces so that the ruffled fringe of the second piece of tissue paper covers the glued portion of the first strip. Work around the cones as best you can. (Caution: tissue paper tends to bleed when it's wet, so be careful not to get it on your clothes.)

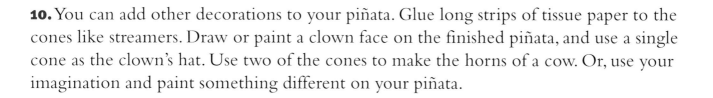

10. You can add other decorations to your piñata. Glue long strips of tissue paper to the cones like streamers. Draw or paint a clown face on the finished piñata, and use a single cone as the clown's hat. Use two of the cones to make the horns of a cow. Or, use your imagination and paint something different on your piñata.

11. After your piñata has dried for another day or two, fill it with prizes and candy, secure the trapdoor with tape, then hang it for your party.

Luminaria are used to decorate entire neighborhoods at Christmastime in Santa Fe.

Luminaria

A family is walking toward a neighbor's house in a small Arizona town. The path to the neighbor's house is lighted by tin lanterns. "This is the festival of **Las Posadas,**" the boy explains. "It's the part of the Christmas story where Joseph and Mary are looking for a place to spend the night."

The lights along the path are called luminarias. The boy continues, "*Las Posadas* begins each year on December 16 and ends on December 25. We go to houses where there are luminarias."

Today, the use of luminarias has spread throughout the United States. People use them to light sidewalks and driveways not only at Christmastime, but for other celebrations as well. Often the luminarias are simply paper bags with candles inside.

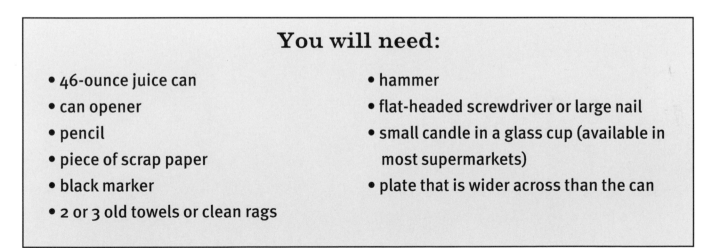

You will need:

- 46-ounce juice can
- can opener
- pencil
- piece of scrap paper
- black marker
- 2 or 3 old towels or clean rags

- hammer
- flat-headed screwdriver or large nail
- small candle in a glass cup (available in most supermarkets)
- plate that is wider across than the can

1. Ask an adult to help. Remove the label from the can. Make sure the inside of the can is clean. Remove one lid with the can opener. Be careful when you throw away the cut-out lid. Its edges will be very sharp.

2. Draw a design on the scrap paper with the pencil to punch onto the luminaria—maybe a bird, or tree, or star. Use dots and dashes rather than solid lines. Copy the pattern onto the can with the marker.

3. Fill the juice can with water and place it in the freezer for 24 hours. The water should be frozen solid when you take it out.

4. Place folded towels or rags on your work surface, and place the can on them. Lay the can on its side. With an adult's help, work quickly (and carefully) to hammer the nail or screwdriver through the dot-and-dash pattern on the can. Hammer just hard enough to pierce the metal. The ice will keep the surface firm until you're done.

5. When you've completed the design, dump out the ice. If it won't come out easily, run the can under hot water. Caution: the pierced metal leaves jagged edges that are very sharp, so don't reach into the can for any reason.

6. To light the luminaria: use a can opener to remove the other lid and throw that away carefully. Place the candle on the middle of the plate, light the candle, and carefully fit your luminaria over it. Enjoy the patterns the light forms.

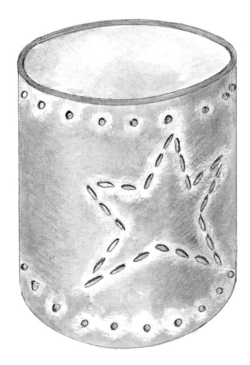

A mariachi group performs at a festival in Texas.

Music and Dance

The music and dance of the American Southwest reveal the mixing of cultures. The Spanish brought their own songs, dances, and musical instruments. As soon as the Spanish arrived in the New World, they were quickly influenced by the Native-American music and dance of the Caribbean islands and of mainland of Central and South America.

By the time the Spanish were well settled in the Southwest, music and dances were a blend of sounds and movements that originally came from Spain, Cuba, other islands in the Caribbean, and Mexico, as well as from the Indian tribes. In addition, African-American rhythms, sounds, and motions quickly fit into the great mixture.

Today, music and dance are important parts of everyday life in the Southwest. They play large roles in popular celebrations and religious ceremonies, as well as community folk dances and social events. Many songs and dances have a boy-meets-girl theme. The Mexican Hat Dance, for example, is performed around a hat, with boys and girls flirting across it.

Traditional dances are an important part of any cultural celebration.

Homemade Banjo

A small school in a New Mexican village is having an autumn festival. All of the children have been invited to make their own musical instruments. An eleven-year-old girl shows the banjo she made out of a cardboard box. "Many families make their own instruments," she says, "and their own costumes. My banjo was fun to make. Wait till you hear the music we make!"

You will need:

- several sheets of newspaper
- small sturdy box with lid, approximately 4 inches wide, 6 or 8 inches long, and 2 inches high
- pencil
- craft knife
- scissors
- acrylic or tempera paints in 2 or 3 bright colors
- small brush, ½ to 1 inch wide
- jar of water

- 2 pieces of stiff cardboard, cut to the same size as the box's long sides (here, 6 or 8 by 2 inches)
- white glue
- 5 large, strong rubber bands, different widths and colors, if possible
- thin piece of wood, like balsa, about 1½-2 inches wide and 12-14 inches long
- 2 pieces of dowel (¼ to ⅜ inch across), each about 3 inches long

1. Spread newspaper over your work surface. Place the box lid on the newspaper, and draw an oval on the inside of the lid with the pencil. Make a slit along the oval with the craft knife, then cut out the oval with the scissors. Younger kids should have an adult help with the craft knife.

2. Turn the lid over and paint it. You can paint one color as the background, let it dry, then add decorations in other colors. Paint the thin piece of wood and the two pieces of dowel in bright colors.

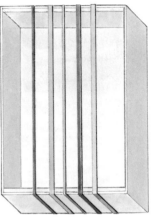

3. Glue the two pieces of stiff cardboard inside each of the box's long sides. This will give the box extra firmness when the rubber bands are strung onto the box.

4. Stretch five rubber bands around the box lengthwise, as shown. All five bands should be placed so they can be seen through the oval on the lid. You can add a little white glue between the rubber bands and where they are stretched across the short sides of the box. Place the lid on the box. The lid should fit firmly. If necessary, add a little glue between the lid and the box.

5. Make a handle. Take the thin piece of wood. Spread glue over about 3 inches of one its sides. Attach the gluey side to the bottom of the box, over the rubber bands.

6. Glue the pieces of dowel across the upper end of the handle, as shown, to look like the frets used to tune a banjo.

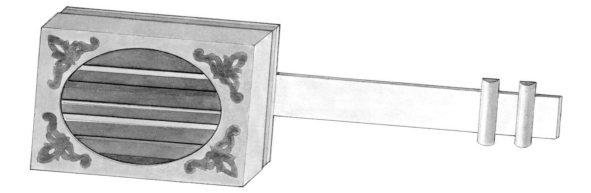

Tambourine

Throughout the Southwest, small musical groups entertain as they stroll through streets, shopping areas, and restaurants. These groups, called **mariachis,** include singers, musicians, and often dancers as well. The musicians' instruments include guitars or banjos, brass horns, and percussion instruments such as tambourines and castanets.

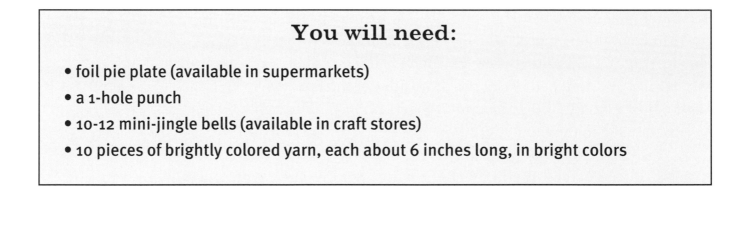

You will need:

- foil pie plate (available in supermarkets)
- a 1-hole punch
- 10-12 mini-jingle bells (available in craft stores)
- 10 pieces of brightly colored yarn, each about 6 inches long, in bright colors

1. Use the hole punch to make ten holes around the rim of the pie plate.

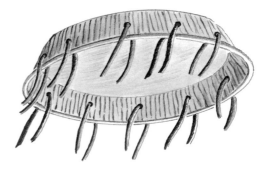

2. Put a piece of yarn through a hole. Don't tie the yarn yet. Thread the yarn through a bell as shown, then tie the yarn. Repeat for all the holes.

3. To play, hold the tambourine in one hand and shake it for a jingling sound, and hit the flat part with your other hand in time to the music.

Glossary

Feast of the Three Kings: A Christian festival in early January.

mariachis: Mexican street band.

missionaries: Catholic priests who came to the New World to bring Christianity to Native Americans.

New World: North and South America—the continents "discovered" by Christopher Columbus.

Old World: The world known to Europeans before Columbus—Europe, Asia, and Africa.

papier-mâché: Material made of paper and glue, used for creating crafts or artwork.

santos: Wood carvings of saints. It means "saints" in Spanish.

Find Out More

Books

Ashabranner, Brent. *Born to the Land: An American Portrait.* New York: G. P. Putnam's Sons, 1989.

Fuentes, Carlos, ed. *Americans: Latino Life in the U.S.* Boston: Little, Brown, 1999.

Ochos, George. *Atlas of Hispanic-American History.* New York: Facts on File, 2001.

Westridge Young Writers Workshop. *Kids Explore America's Hispanic Heritage.* Santa Fe: John Muir Publishing, 1996.

Web Sites:

El Paso Museum of Art
www.elpasoartmuseum.org

Guadalupe Cultural Arts Center
www.guadalupeculturalarts.org

McAllen International Museum
www.rioweb.org/Partners/McAllenIntlMuseum.

Metric Conversion Chart

You can use the chart below to convert from U. S. measurements to the metric system.

Weight
1 ounce = 28 grams
½ pound (8 ounces) = 227 grams
1 pound = .45 kilogram
2.2 pounds = 1 kilogram

Liquid volume
1 teaspoon = 5 milliliters
1 tablespoon = 15 milliliters
1 fluid ounce = 30 milliliters
1 cup = 240 milliliters (.24 liter)
1 pint = 480 milliliters (.48 liter)
1 quart = .95 liter

Length
¼ inch = .6 centimeter
½ inch = 1.27 centimeters
1 inch = 2.54 centimeters

Temperature
100°F = 40°C
110°F = 45°C
350°F = 180°C
375°F = 190°C
400°F = 200°C
425°F = 220°C
450°F = 235°C

About the Author

David C. King is an award-winning author who has written more than forty books for children and young adults, including *Projects About the Eastern Woodland Indians* in the Hands-On History series. He and his wife, Sharon, live in the Berkshires at the junction of New York, Massachusetts, and Connecticut. They have traveled extensively in the American Southwest.

Index